Postcard Stories

POSTCARD STORIES

Short stories by Jan Carson

Illustrated by Benjamin Phillips

THE EMMA PRESS

For Margaret and Diane, my two favourite readers

∽

THE EMMA PRESS

First published in Great Britain in 2017 by the Emma Press Ltd

Text copyright © Jan Carson 2017
Illustrations copyright © Benjamin Phillips 2017

ISBN 978-1-910139-68-4

A CIP catalogue record of this book
is available from the British Library.

Printed and bound in Great Britain
by TJ International, Padstow.

The Emma Press
theemmapress.com
queries@theemmapress.com
Birmingham, UK

*'Your life, so full of people you can hardly
believe it will ever end.'*

From 'One Hundred Characters', a story by
Sam Allingham from his collection *The Great
American Songbook* (A Strange Object, 2016)

☙

Contents

Postcard Stories

Week 1 – January 1ˢᵗ 2015

Susan Fetherston

Every New Year's at midday we meet at the harbour and cast our ghosted bodies into the sea. We are no longer seventeen and, over the years, have progressed from last night's underwear to trunks and t-shirts and, finally, oil-sleek wetsuits, straining to contain our spreading guts. Like soldiers returning from the Front we are fewer with each passing year. This morning we are two – and a handful of bemused children sheltering beneath their anorak hoods.

Afterwards, shivering, we say 'Same time, next year?' and mean, as our fathers must once have meant, 'All good things must come to an end, even the sea.'

Week 2 – January 9th 2015

ALBERT BRIDGE, BELFAST

Tiffany Sahib

January 9th and every third person over the Albert Bridge is running. The marathon looms like the hope of Heaven or Judgement Day. Some are slick as river fish, in all their proper gear. Others make do with tracksuit bottoms and shirts occasionally slept in. The worst lack all conviction. They move from one mile to two, flat-footed in Converse hi-tops, their feet flip-flopping past the station and the market. From a distance they are pedestrian-slow. Up close they have the look of women who return library books half-finished. The noise of them running is the last hand of the applause parting as it cups the silence.

Week 3 – January 18th 2015

BOTANIC AVENUE, BELFAST

Helen Crawford

In the window of Oxfam a volunteer is undressing a red-haired mannequin. Embarrassed, or perhaps complicit, the mannequin looks upwards and to the right, her eyes painted aquarium blue. Her mouth is beginning to peel.

A volunteer lifts her dress gently and slips it over the place where the leg section slots into the torso. A gap the width of an HB pencil circles her hips like a low-slung belt. The volunteer is careful not to upset her further. Upwards then, over a navel-less belly, breasts set and coloured like two pale brown eggs.

'Easy does it,' he says, as he begins to negotiate her neck.

Even through the glass you can see the volunteer is enjoying every awkward second of this until her arms unlock, coming away in his hands like a semi-detached hug.

Week 4 – January 22nd 2015

Hannah McPhillimy

A man in the line for Edinburgh has three inflatable worlds in a plastic bag. He is stopped at the departure gate by an easyJet representative.

'What have you got in the bag?' she asks. It is seven a.m., too early for lipstick, but she is wearing a thick gash of it: bloody red.

'Three worlds,' he replies, and removes them one at a time, clamping them between his feet, because the world is shaped like a soccer ball and inclined to roll if permitted to do so.

'One item of hand luggage only,' she states mechanically, already eyeing up the next offender.

The man proceeds to demonstrate how, with great determination and a little pressure, the world (and all those back-up worlds to come) can be deflated and contained within an overhead luggage locker.

Week 5 – February 1ˢᵗ 2015

LOWER NEWTOWNARDS ROAD, BELFAST

Kelly McCaughrain

On the Lower Newtownards Road there are ginger-bread men scattered across the pavement like the corpse outlines of gunshot victims. Some are crushed; others shattered. A few remain whole and grinning whilst their comrades lie, mere inches away, decapitated by the local dogs. The trail of the dead begins outside Iceland, extending with grim determination past the bus shelter to the ever-open doors of the Bethany chip shop. One loose gingerbread man might be ignored; two dozen or more grate against the proper order of pavements. In these parts it is almost impossible to tell the difference between a funeral and a protest.

Week 6 – February 5th 2015

Cathedral Quarter, Belfast

Claire Buswell

When you were seven years old you threw a dart at a black-haired girl, running away in the garden. The dart lodged and stuck just below her shoulder blade. She fell forwards in the grass. The flight on the dart was red and black and white. These were also the colours of the duvet cover in your parents' bedroom. This was the 80s. Afterwards the dart came away clean as needles. No harm done. You did not tell and neither did she.

You are still wondering if it was ordinary rage which raised your hand to your chin and flung, or something skinnier: the desire for black hair, an older sibling, or a mother waiting by the school gates in a red sports car. Each time you unbend your arm to give blood or turn your ear towards the piercing gun you recall this black-haired girl running away in the garden and hope you have left a mark she can still see.

Week 7 – February 18th 2015

ULSTER HALL, BELFAST

Emma Must

Up from Downpatrick they came to Belfast on the bus. He, in an anorak. She, in a slightly more feminine version of the same anorak. 'Waterproofs', they called them, when the need for a noun arose.

They stopped in Costa for a pair of cloud-topped cappuccinos and split a caramel slice with the dull edge of a teaspoon. Then they trundled on to the lunchtime concert at the Ulster Hall, twenty minutes early for a balcony seat. He, with his ticket printed on the back of an old email. She, with a crossword puzzle printed on the back of hers. It was possible, upon looking closely, to tell his hand from hers, filling in the crossword clues in faint pencil as the bus bumbled its way northwards from Downpatrick.

Week 8 – February 24th 2015

Armagh

Sinéad Morrissey

A provincial Northern Irish library, early evening, and the usual suspects have gathered for a creative writing workshop: two amateur poets, a sci-fi guy in a black t-shirt, a lady who writes letters to her sister in Australia, and that one elderly gentleman who's working on a biography of someone you've never heard of.

You read the Richard Brautigan story about replacing American plumbing with poetry.

'Well,' you say, 'what did we think about that?'

'You've a right nerve on you, wee lassie,' says the elderly gentleman, 'coming down here from Belfast and reading us that sort of stuff. It's not even proper writing.'

It is impossible to tell if he's winding, or genuinely offended.

Week 9 – March 3rd 2015

WHITEABBEY

Ruth Ford

Three writers and a much more useful person gathered for a dinner party. They ate aubergines and couscous impregnated with tequila. Like Jesus, they kept the good wine for pudding. Later, they ended their evening with Bob Dylan and cheese so ripe it might have been shoes. Of course there were anecdotes enough to fill four hours; mostly humorous, occasionally grim. The three writers could not keep themselves from filing away the best of these stories.

'For later use,' they thought, 'in poems and slim novellas.' They were, in this instance only, rivals dashing to be first pen over the finishing line.

'There should be a word,' said the useful person, 'for calling dibs on a good idea. But then again, there are so many ways to write a good idea down: poetry, prose, theatre plays.'

He thought of writing the entire evening into a sonnet but he did not know where to begin, and there were dishes to be done and, afterwards, the coffee.

Week 10 – March 9ᵗʰ 2015

BEDFORD STREET, BELFAST

Claire Spiers

After her children had grown and left home with the express intention of acquiring children all of their own, the old lady began to find the shoe a little empty. Where she'd once loved the novelty of living inside a house shaped like an old-fashioned brogue, she now felt foolish and overly aware of the neighbours staring each time she unlaced her windows.

At the ripe old age of seventy-two, she put her shoe up for sale and moved into a two-bedroom semi on the edge of town. This new home smelt of dishwasher and double-glazed windows. The old woman missed the fleshy stench of damp leather and the floor, which had sprung underfoot like an air-cushioned sole.

When the children came to visit, dragging with them their own reluctant children, there was nowhere to put them all. The old woman complained about the nuisance and secretly relished the familiar pleasure of so many children and not knowing what to do.

Week 11 – March 16th 2015

QUEEN'S FILM THEATRE, BELFAST

Paul Kane

We were not a dog family. We kept chickens for the eggs and, from time to time, a goldfish or two in a cheap plastic bowl. Nor were we close to any families who did dogs. Consequently, all my assumptions about dogs were drawn from Disney movies and Enid Blyton and those individual dogs – mostly Jack Russells – I'd occasionally encounter, anchored to the *Belfast Telegraph* sign outside the VG. Therefore, when the yellow dog approached me in the park with its gums pinking like cooked ham slices, also its teeth bared, I assumed this dog's mouth to be smiling in a peculiarly doggish fashion and extended a friendly hand, which I still miss and, in missing, regret the fact that we were not a dog family.

Week 12 – March 19th 2015

THE SUNFLOWER BAR, BELFAST

Paul Maddern

The twinkle-eyed folk musician Liam Clancy died in 2009. His Aran jumper was made of sterner stuff and persisted well into the next decade. Entering the charity shop circuit in Cork, it migrated north via Limerick and Roscommon, arriving in a Save the Children shop on Belfast's Botanic Avenue just before Christmas 2014.

A young writer, hoping to look more poetic in cable-knit cream, purchased the jumper, wore it to a reading of no real consequence in a local library and, though it itched like a prison blanket, refused to take it off. He imagined that the right kind of girls would take him more seriously in such a sweater. Besides, there was something of Clancy haunting every stitch of his pullover and, charmed by the grip of songs he was too late to remember, the writer found that his stories now came easier when sung loudly in low-roofed rooms.

Week 13 – March 27th 2015

EAST BELFAST

Dan Bolger

I saw on Facebook that you spent the weekend in Bournemouth. It is too early in the season for British seaside resorts and I cannot help but love you for choosing Bournemouth over other, more continental, cities. The snow has barely melted and there are only locals in the street, their skin tanned potato-tough from that biting wind. The shops, which sell candy rock and novelty hats, have yet to raise their summer shutters. There is no ice cream to be had for love nor money.

In the pictures you are wearing a hat and scarf, two coats (blanketed one on top of the other), and the mittens I gave you for Christmas last year. I hope they are joined together still, with string; the length of them snaking up one sleeve and down the other, circling your back where my arms used to meet.

Week 14 – April 3rd 2015

Botanic Avenue, Belfast

Tom Stutzmann

This is not quite Ireland proper/is not the Mainland/ is certainly not Europe in the Continental sense. This is particularly true on the Friday before Easter when alcohol may only be purchased (legally) between the evening hours of five and eleven.

'Good Friday,' the hard-drinking men and women of Belfast are heard to exclaim around about last orders, 'tell me what's so bloody good about it?' (They say this every year as if they've only just thought of it.) The average Ulsterman is a stoic breed. Hardened by rain and other damp sorrows he has come to view life's limits as a challenge.

Good Friday will only be good if he puts the effort in. He begins drinking at five and, when the taps tighten against him, takes his resolve outside to a bus shelter where he consumes six cans of Coors Light in less than an hour, pausing only to piss it out against a lamp-post. By closing time he is a ghost of himself. It is no longer Good Friday and he cannot remember the word for resurrection.

Week 15 – April 13th 2015

Albertbridge Road, Belfast

Hannah Mill

At the junction where the Ravenhill Road meets the edge of the Albert Bridge, a well-dressed gentleman falls into step beside her. Heel to toe, heel to toe, lunch bags swinging like metronomes, they shoulder each other across the bridge and past the station. They do not speak but she glances sideways from time to time, anxious not to fall behind his proud nose.

Reflected in the bus shelter's glass walls they are condiment bottles, cutlery, chess pieces; two different items, paired through association. People driving past in cars and buses might presume them a couple. She has not yet seen enough of him to decide whether this would be a good, or ridiculous, thing.

They part ways outside St George's Market. Her cheek is cold and dry where he has not kissed her. Later, at her desk, she wonders what she has not packed for his lunch. Tonight, she will couple another man across the Albert Bridge, or perhaps, if the lights are unduly cautious, a woman instead.

Week 16 – April 19th 2015

BELMONT ROAD, EAST BELFAST

Jonny Scott

In the autumn of last year we bought a fixer-upper on the edge of Saintfield. Imagine our surprise when we opened the door to our new home, only to discover that the house came with a cooker, a washing machine, and the previous resident installed in the living room.

At first we decorated around her, avoiding the central section of the living room, where the old lady had hunkered down with a year's supply of *The People's Friend*. Later, we would grow accustomed to her, call her Mags (though we'd no idea of her given name), rest our drinks on her lap and lean against her while recounting our anecdotes at cocktail parties and informal soirees. She neither objected nor seemed particularly glad to be included.

'I'm not leaving,' she'd say from time to time as if we were asking or even insisting. 'It wouldn't be home if I wasn't here.'

Week 17 – April 29th 2015

Newtownards Road, East Belfast

Lois Kennedy

The last power ballad on the planet did not realize it was alone until it was too late. Behind its wet drums, synthesizers and triumphant bass line it was impossible to hear anything else.

The last power ballad on the planet featured love and air punching, not giving up, and everything being alright in the end. (In this, and other aspects, it was remarkably similar to all the other power ballads which had preceded it.) The last power ballad on the planet was not to be defeated. Listening to itself at high volume in its own bedroom, it began to feel its self-confidence returning. It chanced a saxophone solo. This looked particularly good in the wardrobe mirror. It followed up with a key change.

'Nothing's going to stop us now,' thought the last power ballad on the planet before remembering that there was no longer an 'us' in power balladery. This was too sad for its synthesizers to bear. There were not enough acoustic guitars in the world to compensate for its loss.

Week 18 – May 6th 2015

HOLYWOOD ROAD, EAST BELFAST

Karen Vaughan

The photoshopped novelist has teeth like a toothpaste commercial, skin like the exposed torso of a 1980s Barbie doll. The photoshopped novelist prefers leaning against exposed brick walls, holds her chin as if it is an overfull teacup, thinks about important things happening just out of shot. The photoshopped novelist heard on *Woman's Hour* that you shouldn't wear dangly earrings (too distracting, too much of a cliché) and consequently doesn't. She wears black on all occasions, even on holidays, and is warmer in her armpits than she'd ever admit. The photoshopped novelist dreams in black and oh-so-forgiving white, practises holding notebooks with intent, and reads Bukowski on the bus as this is easier than telling men to 'piss off'. The photoshopped novelist once saw herself reflected in the window of Topshop. It was a sunny day. She could not hold her tears in.

Week 19 – May 7th 2015

Queen's Film Theatre, Belfast

Amy Boles

William goes to the pictures once a week on Thursday. He is not fussy about which movie he sees, though quieter films or those with subtitles are usually more appealing. He arrives late and sits beside someone – usually a single someone – who looks as if they have been waiting to see this movie all week. During the previews and opening credits William does a credible impression of an ordinary cinema-goer. However, once the film begins in earnest he really cuts loose. He coughs. He checks the time on his watch, then his mobile phone, then his watch again. He eats noisily. He coughs some more, plays with the zipper on his anorak so it makes the sound of ripped paper. He sighs. (William finds that sighing is the best way to drive his fellow audience members bat crazy.) He could not care one jot for the action onscreen. It is the angry, angry people on either side who amuse William, who justify the ticket price.

Week 20 – May 16th 2015

DUNADRY

Mary Dixon

The bride is small at the top and wider at the bottom like a pyramid, or a toilet paper lady. Coming in or out of a room she must turn sideways to accommodate her train. The bride is named Catherine but looking at her it is hard not to assume she has been called Cathy in youth and Cat since the age of seventeen. She is at least thirty-seven now but her dress is ten years younger.

There is a stain like the Red Hand of Ulster simmering across the backside of this dress as if the bride has sat herself down in something bloody, as if she has thrown red wine over her own shoulder in some strange parody of that lucky salt ritual, as if someone with no sense (her father perhaps) has placed his hand on her and given her a good hefty shove into the next chapter.

Week 21 – May 27th 2015

BELMONT ROAD, EAST BELFAST

Eleanor Kyle

The Wilsons could not afford more than one baby. Nor did they believe in only children.

'It's cruel,' said Mrs. Wilson, 'bringing a child up without another child for company.'

When their baby was old enough to sit up they placed him in a small room, mirrored on all four sides.

'Look at all the mirror babies,' they said, 'so many friends to play with.'

They took great comfort in the way their baby talked to his reflection as if the children in the mirror were real. Later, when he was sixteen or seventeen and the mirror room had been demolished to make way for a home office, the boy had vague memories of siblings. He presumed them, all but himself, dead and did not ask, but there was a sadness inside him like a two-sided mirror.

Week 22 – May 28th 2015

DONEGAL SQUARE, BELFAST

Sam and Emily Moore

There is some confusion in the line for the 28A. An elderly lady in a coral anorak has stuck her head, turtle-like, from beneath her umbrella's brim to announce 'Margaret's not doing well at all.' She asks the next elderly lady down if there's been any change in Margaret's condition.

This one's wearing a pink anorak and says 'They're just waiting on Margaret now.'

Which causes a third anorak (navy blue, nautical-themed) to chip in with news from the frontline: 'Margaret's just passed.'

'No,' argues the original anorak, 'that can't be right for I was only after talking to Margaret's John.' She sets her bag-for-life down on the pavement as if to prove she's here for the duration.

The dots are duly joined and it transpires that there is more than one Margaret dying in East Belfast today. All three anoraks shuffle on to the 28A and keep their hoods up all the way down the Newtownards Road. It is unclear whether they are in mourning or just worried about their hair.

Week 23 – June 6th 2015

Botanic Avenue, Belfast

Diana Decaris Champa

We did not work in English so we tried translation. I was particularly keen on French but soon realized that a harsh truth is just as heavy when delivered with romantic intonation. Architecture was your best attempt at explaining us yet you could not decide if we were detached, semi-detached or stubbornly terraced. Soon our very foundations were not strong enough to support us. Sign language was equally disappointing.

'I feel like we're just playing rock, scissors, paper here,' I said with my hands, and all you saw was a fist, falling in the most violent fashion.

In the end we were reduced to quadratic equations; less than or equal to everything we had previously been.

Week 24 – June 13th 2015

BOTANIC AVENUE, BELFAST

Glori Gray

'What's the difference?' she thought, and went to the Poundshop, where the dishwasher tablets were cheaper. She kept her mother's change and felt no guilt.

Though the brand was identical to the dishwasher tablets they normally used, the writing on the packet was in a foreign language – Polish or Romanian, the words recognisably Eastern. She stored the box under the sink with the other cleaning products and hoped her mother would not notice.

Her mother did not notice. The dishes were no more nor less clean than usual but there were tiny foreign fingerprints on the cutlery and a strange taste off the cups, like sadness in a foreign film. This persisted even after a second and third rinse. She could not shift her thirst with these cups no matter how much she drank.

Week 25 – June 23rd 2015

ULSTER HALL, BELFAST

Anthony Quinn

When I grow up I want to be a player in a paper orchestra. This is similar to being a player in an ordinary orchestra except the instruments are extremely affordable, as they are not made of brass or wood or any kind of permanent material. I will be able to become a violinist then, just a few weeks later, a trumpet player, a cellist or even a banger of over-sized drums. Furthermore, the noise made by a paper orchestra is nothing near the racket generated by an everyday orchestra, even in rehearsal. The sound of a paper orchestra is like the memory of a song heard once in passing, or rain behind glass, or the noise human breath will make catching on the inside of a woollen scarf. Paper orchestras are all the more precious because they are disposable and because they are also subject to the subtle shifts of wind and gentle wear.

Week 26 – June 25th 2015

CATALYST ARTS, BELFAST

Aislinn Clarke

The year we were married Peter and I rented a second-floor apartment on the East Side. To the left of us lived a woman with lizards; to the right, two schoolteachers who only made noise at weekends. Directly above us was a young Mexican man in training for the regional heats of Mr. Universe. He wore shorts at all times, even in winter, and spent his evenings lifting weights in the privacy of his own kitchen. We could picture the cut of him: legs spread, arms wide, heaving half his own body weight while the television mounted over the breakfast bar played *Baywatch* re-runs. The sound of his weights leaving the ground was inaudible. Their returns registered in the bedroom below like earthquakes and other signs of the end times.

Week 27 – July 3rd 2015

ALBERTBRIDGE ROAD, BELFAST

Kara Nelson

The Tall Ships arrived in Belfast yesterday. They were not as tall as we'd been led to believe. We thought you might be able to see them from space or, at very least, Cave Hill. This was not the case. You had to be right under the masts and looking up to achieve the illusion of tallness. And, there were fewer of them than we'd been promised; something to do with the smallness of our harbour and health and safety legislation.

'Still,' said the people who were captains, or whatever one calls the drivers of ships these days, 'this is a remarkably small country. Surely everything must seem big and tall and much, much more impressive when you're used to so very little.'

The old perspective argument.

We've heard this one before. The punchline is always less is more in your case. It does not hold water. We know this for a fact. Belfast once harboured boats big as city blocks. These boats were considered equally grand from every foreign perspective, including the ocean floor.

Week 28 – July 11ᵗʰ 2015

BELMONT ROAD, EAST BELFAST

Jonny Currie

There are small, jungle-living monkeys in the new Ikea advert. Look at them eating bananas straight from the fridge, turning the taps on and off with reckless abandon and smashing the crockery like there is an endless supply of affordable cups and plates. They are having a jolly old time, these little monkeys in their jungle kitchen, and yet you cannot enter into their joy. You are reminded of the red-faced monkey in the National Geographic advert, squatting unhappily in some Amazonian river. You see this monkey constantly. It has the face of your father, sad and frowning as if utterly devastated. You find this advert impossible to watch and, by association, all monkey-based advertising.

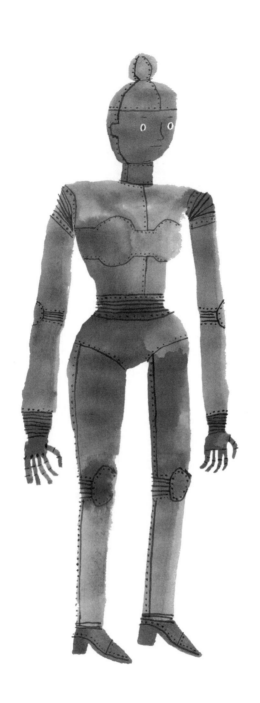

Week 29 – July 21st 2015

LINENHALL STREET, BELFAST

Becca Dean

I am making a robot of myself. It will look exactly like me, only silver. People I know will see the robot of me in Tesco or on the bus and will be struck by its resemblance to me and also its shininess. They will see themselves reflected in its face or on the smooth slope of its back. They will automatically stop to check their hair, tucking wayward strands behind their ears as if the robot of me is a mere mirror, only there for their convenience. The robot of me will not be funny or write stories or be good at conversation with wine. I will be particularly careful to ensure the robot is a dull dinner party guest for fear that my friends might begin to prefer its company over mine. The robot of myself will exist to do things I do not enjoy doing such as tax returns and going to funerals. I will not bother to give the robot of myself a name.

Week 30 – July 22nd 2015

BOTANIC AVENUE, BELFAST

Sophie Collins

When it came to the final number and everyone in the audience was asked to sing along with 'Somewhere Over the Rainbow', two people did not know the words. Or perhaps it would be more accurate to say, two people only knew the phrase 'somewhere over the rainbow' and the accompanying melody. During the other sections of the verse and chorus these two people opened and closed their mouths silently in time to the piano. From a distance it was impossible to tell that they were not producing sound, though there was an almost unperceivable time lapse between their jaws and the jaws of those audience members sitting to their left and right. Both these people had had rather disappointing childhoods and this was why they did not know the words to 'Somewhere Over the Rainbow.' The memory of their disappointing childhoods came back to them as they lip synched and both, without consulting one another, determined not to cry and also to Google the lyrics as soon as they got home.

Week 31 – August 1ˢᵗ 2015

Ikea, Belfast

Joan Weber

I left my father in Ikea. He was too old to go on. When I showed him the living room department – all those armchairs in lines and grids like a street map and right next door the same again in beds – he looked straight into my eyes and I could see the tiredness had settled into him. It was too much to expect him to make it to kitchens or bathrooms; the lighting department was already well beyond him.

'Sit down here,' I said, lowering him into a brown, leather armchair, a kind of Scandinavian take on Eames. 'You have done well,' I said, 'so well, to make it this far.'

I could see he was glad of the rest, glad to have the expectation lifted from him. I turned away from my father and progressed on to bedrooms and kitchens. I did not look back. I did not return for him. There is only one route through Ikea.

Week 32 – August 11th 2015

DUBLIN ROAD, BELFAST

Claire Shaw

There are feral children living inside the Dublin Road Cinema; three of them. They do not have names as such and, having learnt all their language from the movies, have come to call themselves Disney and Pixar and Bat Man (Bat Man being the smallest of the three and the only male). They cannot remember how they arrived there at the Dublin Road Cinema but they do not want to leave. They scuttle from screen to screen when the lights are down, avoiding the ushers and eating popcorn in handfuls straight from the floor. During the day they sleep, curled like pretzels, beneath the folding seats. Their skin is like milk or paper, from never having been outside. When they see themselves in the bathroom mirrors, wild-haired and white, they touch their faces and touch the faces of their siblings. They do not pass right through each other. It is a relief to know they are not yet ghosts. Ghosts are things which end badly in every movie they have ever seen.

Week 33 – August 16th 2015

SALT ISLAND, STRANGFORD LOUGH

Erika Meitner

Over the hills we go, seven poets, a picnic basket, and a handful of children who are carrying sticks and collecting pocketfuls of bone-white shells. We have come in search of seals. We have discovered no seals, only thistles and nettles which are not kind to summer sandals or bare ankles. We line along the brow of the hill and peer across the Lough towards Ards and Scrabo beyond. Still there are no seals, though we almost convince ourselves that those black lines cresting the curled waves are their backs or raised heads. We are not disappointed to have been here. It has required bicycles and cars, two boats and much walking, though there are still no seals. Every inch of the journey has been worth it, just to stand here on this hill casting our long shadows across the Lough like a net for all our absent creatures.

Week 34 – August 19th 2015

ULSTER HALL, BELFAST

Catherine Gander

I thought the first things to be forgotten would be the hard facts: the Battle of Hastings, the freezing point of water, how many days I might expect to encounter in February during a leap year. This was not true. The first things which slipped free were feelings: the ill-defined anxiety of whether a room was there for the entering or the leaving, who I loved and how much this love could be leant upon when a name could not be found to pair with it, how I'd arrived at this place with the curtains drawn and it not yet gone three. There was not even a way to say that I had forgotten these things; only a jumble of words too long or too short for the job and a clenching of fists when the words would not come. Even then, the hard facts remained and I could say with certainty: 1066 and zero degrees and 28 days clear, 29 in each leap year, which was a ludicrous way to let you know I was lost, like using a fork to spoon soup.

Week 35 – August 27th 2015

BALLYMENA

Andrew Farmer

I am trying to help the doctor. I have read somewhere that a local GP is allocated just 8 (or is it 11?) minutes per consultation with each patient. I am planning to be in and out of the surgery in less than 5. I have always been an overachiever.

'This is where it hurts,' I say, lifting my sweater to reveal the sore spot marked on my ribcage with a felt tip pen.

'I think I am allergic to citrus fruits,' I say, pointing to my face which is swollen from the lime slices I have been sucking in the waiting room.

'I probably have a kidney stone,' I say and hand the doctor a list of my symptoms carefully printed next to a Wikipedia article on kidney stones.

Even though we still have 3 allocated minutes left, the doctor does not seem as pleased as I thought he'd be. Perhaps I have stolen all the best bits of being a doctor. All he has left are prescriptions and updating my patient notes online. A secretary could easily do this. Maybe he is even wondering what he went to medical school for.

Week 36 – September 2nd 2015

KNOCKNAGONEY, EAST BELFAST

Bri Farren

I am practising so in the future I will be the kind of professional journalist who is taken seriously by colleagues and members of the public alike. I am almost always carrying a notebook and pen, thereby giving the impression that I am keen and ready to capture the next big story. I am performing ordinary tasks such as cereal eating and teeth brushing with set deadlines in mind. This will help me achieve greater efficiency within the time limits afforded to professional journalists. I am asking demanding questions of everyone I meet such as: 'Were you happy as a child?' (to the girl on the till at Tesco) and 'Why is your face like that?' (to the man who serves me coffee in the morning). I am wearing flat shoes. I am buying a trenchcoat. I am telling myself quite firmly that the truth is the only thing which truly matters. I am practising hard. Sometimes, when I look in the mirror I no longer see myself. Instead, I see a professional journalist wearing my face.

Week 37 – September 15th 2015

DONEGAL SQUARE, BELFAST

Lynne McMordie

When I came back from the shops you were in the garden listening to the trees. When I say you were listening to the trees, I mean you were actually listening to them, resting an upturned whiskey glass against the sycamore's trunk like an old-school detective eavesdropping through the bedroom wall.

'What are you doing?' I asked.

'Listening to the trees,' you said.

'What are the trees saying?' I asked.

You shrugged your shoulders sharply and said, 'How should I know? I don't speak tree.'

'What's the point in listening to them then?'

'It makes the trees feel good to know there's someone prepared to listen,' you said, 'even if that person doesn't understand them.'

I didn't have the words to say I know how those trees feel, which wasn't quite true, because it has been months since you last listened to me, even through a glass.

Week 38 – September 20th 2015

Paddy Brown

Last night we met a Spanish penguin floating round the Cornmarket. It was raining, as it almost always is in Belfast, and he didn't have an umbrella.

'I am looking for a traditional music session,' he said in broken English. He was on a mini-break from Madrid.

We took the penguin to the Duke of York. There are usually trad sessions there on a Sunday afternoon. It took almost half an hour to walk across town, on account of his very short legs.

When we arrived at the Duke the bouncer told us, quite firmly, that penguins weren't permitted on the premises.

So we said, 'He's on a mini-break and isn't this city supposed to welcome visitors now?'

'Ah,' said the bouncer, 'I'm sorry. I thought you were a local penguin. We make an exception here for tourist penguins. Come on, on in. You'll be wanting a Guinness, I presume?'

The Spanish penguin had a pint of Guinness, and then a second pint. By the third it was clear that penguins cannot hold their drink for he was on the table doing his own penguiny version of the flamenco and taking photos for Facebook.

Week 39 – September 24th 2015

Holywood

Jen and Paul McClean

In the backseat of my car there is a horse and a tunnel. The horse is not a real horse; it is only a child's horse for rocking. The tunnel is very real. It is currently bound tightly with strings, but when these strings are released it will immediately unfold and reveal itself to be almost two metres in length. It is all the colours of the primary rainbow. At one end of the tunnel is the future and, at the other end, the past.

The horse has not yet ventured into the tunnel but it might. The horse is not afraid of confronting its past, nor its future, nor the futuristic things such as robot horses or sleek, metal wings which it might encounter in the future. It is only afraid of becoming lodged in the tunnel and remaining there like an awkward lump in the throat, stuck between the future and the past, which is another name for the present; the present being a darkish place that does not permit looking forwards or back.

Week 40 – September 28ᵗʰ 2015

ULSTER HALL, BELFAST

Laura Conlon

Myra has lost her teeth. She had them this morning in a glass beside her bed. Then, later on the bus into town, they were in her mouth and on a plate beside her soup bowl at lunch. Then back into her mouth though, opening and closing her mouth now, Myra finds they are no longer there. There is nothing with which to hold the walls of her mouth up and her cheeks are falling in like paper bags crumpling against their own emptiness. Myra has lost her teeth. She has also lost the word for teeth and so she points and points again at her open mouth, all the time looking like a woman who has lost a very vital thing. Her friends understand. They turn the place upside down looking for Myra's lost teeth. They are not in her handbag. They are not in the ladies' toilets. They are not on the coffee table with the scones and the side plates.

'Myra,' they say, smiling, smiling, smiling like warm blankets or scarves, 'are you sure you didn't leave your teeth at home?'

And Myra suddenly has a picture in her head of teeth bubbling in a water glass but she cannot remember if this picture is today, yesterday, or something from a film she once saw on television.

Week 41 – October 7ᵗʰ 2015

Sᴛᴅᴇɴʜᴀᴍ Dʀɪᴠᴇ, Eᴀsᴛ Bᴇʟꜰᴀsᴛ

Suzanne Crooks

You were born with a bird's egg grasped firmly in your right hand. It wasn't big enough to be a chicken's. It was pale blue with freckles like the eggs you sometimes come across in woodland nests. You don't remember being born with a bird's egg in your fist or how it got there; why it hadn't cracked under the pressure of your fingers or the force of being born. It is a mystery to you, like breathing or knowing a thing you have not been told.

After you were born they took the bird's egg out of your hand and kept it for days under a heat lamp, but it did not hatch. Eventually they opened it, cracked its thin shell against a spoon and tipped it – yolk and all – into a teacup. There was a little dot, like the red of an eye in photographs. It was swimming in the yolk. It looked up at them and did not blink. Why would it?

So there you newly were, with an egg in your hand, with an eye in this egg, like a set of Russian dolls or how we all are, secretly, inside.

Week 42 – October 12th 2015

BEDFORD STREET, BELFAST

Colin Dardis

The man who lives in the apartment directly above ours has recently taken up drumming. He only practises during daylight hours. He is a reasonably considerate kind of man. I think his name is Bill. The sound of his drums stamping and settling against our roof is like thunder or something more precise. Claire says it is like dancing, but I have passed this man in the corridor en route to the recycling bins or the communal postbox and the simile will not stick. He is no dancer. He is not even an elegant walker.

I say, 'The sound of his drums is like Morse code muttering through the ceiling tiles,' and Claire likes the idea of this.

'What's he saying?' she asks. 'Is it a cry for help?'

Because she is prettier by half when she smiles, I humour her and reply, 'Oh no, it's not a cry for help. It's the start of a really great conversation.'

Then we lift brooms and tennis racquets and golf umbrellas and tap our pretend Morse into the ceiling. 'Thump. Tadump. Thump.' Which, when translated, means, 'Hey, Bill, hope you're as happy as we are.'

Week 43 – October 19th 2015

BELMONT ROAD, EAST BELFAST

Matthew O'Neill

The houses in our neighbourhood have only recently been given recycling bins. This is probably because we do not live in a city and the Council have made certain assumptions about our ability to engage with environmental issues such as polar ice caps, carbon footprints and sticking our potato peelings in the green food bin. We are proving the Council very, very wrong.

We are placing our cardboard in one bin, our paper in the other. We are separating glass bottles from those made of plastic. We are faithfully placing our bins out for collection every second Tuesday, on the pavement. And, if we sometimes slip the odd non-traditional item into the recycling bin – secrets, dirty jokes, ex-wives, unwanted pets – it is only because we truly believe that somewhere, in a city or small town much like ours, someone else will see the greater good in these items, will get more out of them than we ever could. This is how we've come to define recycling.

Week 44 – October 23rd 2015

Belmont Tower, East Belfast

Kate Bryan

Dear C.S. Lewis,

You will be disappointed to hear that while I climbed into my wardrobe and went feeling around for the portal to another world, I did not encounter Narnia, only the back of my wardrobe (which is made of plywood) and some coat hangers jangling together like biscuit tin lids.

Do you suppose my wardrobe is to fault, C.S.? It's only a flat-pack one from Ikea. It's not even that big. Or was it the absence of fur coats which made all the difference? I keep summer dresses in my wardrobe; cardigans, skirts, and the kind of blouses which can't be folded for fear of wrinkling. These items, when pressed upon, do not part with the same soft animal shrug. They do not smell like old ladies at the theatre. But no one owns a fur coat for real these days, Mr. Lewis. Everyone considers such articles cruel; even the people who can actually afford to buy them.

Besides, C.S. Lewis, we both know it wasn't the wardrobe or the clothes which kept me out of Narnia. I simply did not believe enough.

Week 45 – November 3rd 2015

Victoria Square, Belfast

Susan Picken

'If your drink doesn't make you happy we'll make you another,' I read aloud, pointing to the sign above the barista's head. It's been there, right behind him, with the toastie machine and the coffee syrups, for so long now that he's forgotten all about it. Occasionally someone refers to the sign when their latte is not as hot as they'd like it to be, or their cappuccino is burnt, but most people are too polite to complain. Not me!

'I finished my coffee and it didn't make me happy,' I tell the barista.

He asks if it was too hot, too cold, too weak, too strong?

I say, 'No, no, no, there's nothing wrong with this coffee. It just didn't make me happy. I am still as unhappy as I was before drinking this coffee.'

Then I begin to cry and because the barista does not know what to do he gets the manager. The manager offers me another coffee and a muffin (with the implication of a free panini if I'll just stop crying over the pastry counter). I take their muffin and their free coffee but neither item makes me happy. There are only so many free coffees a person can drink before admitting that a hot beverage cannot cure loneliness or grief or general melancholy.

Week 46 – November 12th 2015

BOTANIC AVENUE, BELFAST

Charlotte Lewis

When the removal men eventually arrived it took them less than an hour to empty the apartment. They filled a van with our furniture stacked upside down and sideways so it fit together like a tower of interlocking Jenga bricks. We took a moment to walk through the empty rooms. This had been our home for almost ten years and, while we'd outgrown it, it was not as if we'd fallen out of love with the kitchen and the living room and the master bedroom with its tiny en suite.

As we passed from room to empty room we began to notice that although our tables and chairs were already half way to Lisburn, the shadows of our furniture remained, lingering softly on the carpet. You thought it was dirt and scuffed at it gently with the edge of your shoe, hoping to blend it into the rug. I thought the floor had faded around our furniture. It was a bright apartment, and over the years the sun had turned the wallpaper pastel in certain places.

Neither of us was right.

These were not stains nor faded patches. These were the sad ghosts of our sofa, our coffee table and our Ikea bookcase. They did not want to leave this apartment. They preferred to stay behind and haunt it. They, like us, had been terribly happy here.

Week 47 – November 16th 2015

ULSTER HALL, BELFAST

Sandra Rutherford

When we were sixteen years old they sent us to dance lessons down in the city centre. The girls went into one room. We boys went into another. We learnt how to lead. We learnt how to hold the rhythm like the rhythm was a fine line and, on either side of it, a sheer drop. We were taught not to apologise to the girls. If we stood upon their toes it was because their toes had not stepped backwards or forwards at the correct time. We did not dance with each other. This would have been ludicrous; almost grown men sweeping each other round the dance floor by the wrists. We danced in lines instead, tiptoeing round our ghost partners as our arms reached out towards them and our feet played footsy with their absent shoes.

When we were accomplished enough to deserve partners they took us into the room with the girls and put us together in pairs. We did not need to speak to these girls. Our feet already knew what to say. We were like a two-part harmony singing together for the very first time.

Week 48 – November 22nd 2015

ULSTER MUSEUM, BELFAST

Emma Logan

The museum was not like any museum she'd visited before. She stopped one of the guards at the door and asked in a whisper (for she didn't want one of the other visitors to overhear and presume her ignorant) what sort of a museum this was.

'This is a museum of all the things we are trying to forget,' replied the guard.

Everything made much more sense then. The gilt frames with ordinary objects such as guns or wedding bands suspended against the gallery walls. The interactive grief display. The glass cabinets of children's shoes and war and stuffed dogs and sepia-tinted photographs of old people in stern collars. The dead people posed like sculptures. Even the empty frames made sense to her; here were things already forgotten and passed from memory.

She thought she might visit this museum again and wondered if it was possible to donate some small item such as a book or a phrase he'd once said angrily to her in the street. She stopped the same guard to ask about donations and he looked at her blankly with polite disinterest as if he'd already forgotten her face. He was a very efficient guard, the best in the whole museum.

Week 49 – December 2nd 2015

DONEGAL SQUARE, BELFAST

Molly Pearl Owen

Yesterday I wore my new shoes to work. Several of my colleagues commented on how nice they were with their shiny buckles and their soft, brown toes.

'Oh, these old things,' I said, 'I've had them for ages.'

This wasn't exactly true. But the inability to take a compliment is wired into us Northern folk like the propensity to ignore rain or drink tea, to take the wrong end of the stick and beat our neighbours round the head with it.

Which leads me to a conversation I once overheard on the bus between Knock and Castlereagh.

'What a beautiful-looking wee baby,' said this one older lady to the woman sitting opposite her with a buggy.

The woman with the buggy, pre-conditioned as she was to deflect compliments of all kinds, did not miss a beat, nor chance to look at her sleeping child for fear of nurturing an arrogant streak. 'Oh this old thing,' she replied curtly, 'sure, I've had her for ages.'

As I said, it runs through us all like a coastal seam, this fear of leaning too far into a good or kindly thing.

Week 50 – December 10th 2015

Linenhall Street, Belfast

Martin and Lucy Cathcart Froden

This morning I read that Kay Ryan poem, the one about the fourth Wise Man who disliked travel and preferred his own bed to the open road, which made me think of the shepherd who went off for a quick wee at exactly the wrong angelic moment, and all the people who, upon hearing there was only one portion of loaves and fish to split between so many, went home to fix their own sandwiches, and the guests who drank themselves blind beneath the tables long before the water turned wineish, and, of course, the disciples, who were almost always asleep in boat bottoms and gardens and other comfortable spots, missing the point of everything. And finally I arrived at myself and the very many times I have decided to stay in, watching re-runs of *Morse* and *Poirot*, reading paperback novels in bed, whilst in the streets and bars and staged rooms of this city miracles are miracling away and I am only afterwards hearing about them on Facebook.

Week 51 – December 18th 2015

Week 51 – December 18th 2015

ORMEAU ROAD, BELFAST

Damian Smyth

This morning the Loch Ness monster died. It was to have been her nine hundred thousandth new day and, while she was a great old one for rounding up, she did not think she could bear another hundred thousand wakenings just to hit the square million.

It was not guns which killed her in the end, nor old age, or even the skeptics trying to disprove her with their sonar machines and special cameras. It was, instead, a very specific kind of loneliness which caused her to draw breath and hold that breath until her big lungs sank and all the seeing went out of her eyes. It was the loneliness of being left behind after everyone else has gone home.

By this evening the Loch Ness monster will have begun to disappear; her monster belly caving in upon itself, her skin slipping loose and bones unclasping to bury themselves in the gritty silt. Smaller and more ordinary creatures will strip her bare with their mouths and teeth.

Tomorrow there will be nothing left to prove the Loch Ness monster has ever been. This will have no impact whatsoever on those individuals (both local and international) who can believe in things unseen. They will continue to hope for her arched neck, humping every time the loch rises.

Week 52 – December 26th 2015

St George's Market, Belfast

Hugh Odling-Smee

Every year during the month leading up to Christmas, Eleanor takes a stall at St George's Market and sells disappointment in small, hand-made bottles. It is mostly locals who buy from her. The tourists tend to skip straight from the felt handbag stall on her left to the organic candles on her right, barely pausing to register the little glass bottles lined across Eleanor's table.

She stocks any number of different disappointments: the disappointment of an unsupportive parent, the disappointment of a homely child, the disappointment of being alone or not nearly alone enough, the disappointment of cats, good wine, box sets and religion, the dry disappointment of Christmas Day evening which is easily the most popular product on her stall. Customers seem to know without asking exactly the right disappointment to buy.

Eleanor only sells disappointment at Christmas. She could not afford the fees for an all-year stall. Besides, during the rest of the year people do not require an excuse for the way they feel kind of hopeless first thing in the morning. The sun is up or down and one day follows the next and what is there to be particularly happy about? At Christmas people are expected to sparkle and when they cannot muster the guts it helps to have a bottle to point to, to be able to say, 'I was absolutely fine till I took this.'

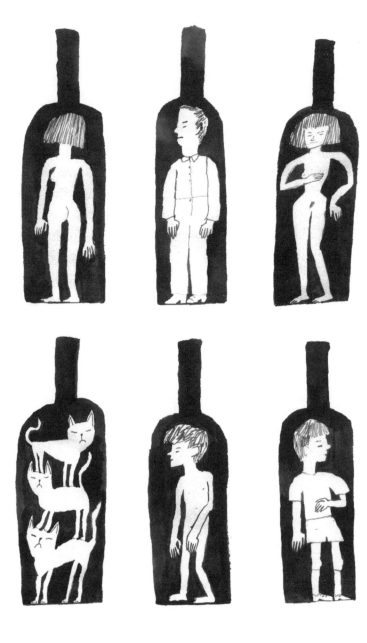

Acknowledgements

The epigraph on page v, from *The Great American Songbook* by Sam Allingham (A Strange Object, 2016), is used with kind permission from the author.

About the author

Jan Carson is a writer based in Belfast, Northern Ireland. Her first novel, *Malcolm Orange Disappears*, was published by Liberties Press in 2014, followed by a short story collection, *Children's Children,* in 2016. Her short story 'Settling' was included in the anthology *The Glass Shore: Short Stories by Women Writers from the North of Ireland* (New Island, 2016), which won the BGEIBA Irish Book of the Year Award in 2016. Her short stories have been broadcast on BBC Radio 3 and 4 and published in journals including *Storm Cellar, Banshee, Harper's Bazaar* and *The Honest Ulsterman.* In 2014 she was a recipient of the Arts Council NI Artist's Career Enhancement Bursary.

About the illustrator

Artist and illustrator Benjamin Phillips lives in St Leonards-on-Sea and shares a studio in Hastings with his partner and dog. Benjamin finds inspiration in human interaction, the humour and turmoil of everyday life and the joy of repetition. His debut graphic novel, *Peanutborough Cucumberland*, was published by Log Press in 2012, and he has worked for clients such as *The New York Times*, Virgin Media, the Jerwood Gallery and Wichita Records.

benjaminphillips.co.uk

THE EMMA PRESS

small press, big dreams

The Emma Press is an independent publisher based in Birmingham, UK, dedicated to producing beautiful, thought-provoking books. It was founded in 2012 by Emma Wright. Having been shortlisted in both 2014 and 2015, the Emma Press won the Michael Marks Award for Poetry Pamphlet Publishers in 2016.

The Emma Press is passionate about making poetry welcoming and accessible. In 2015 they received a grant from Arts Council England to travel around the country with *Myths and Monsters*, a tour of poetry readings and workshops for children. They are often on the lookout for new writing and run regular calls for submissions.

Sign up to the Emma Press newsletter to hear about their events, books and calls for submissions.

theemmapress.com
emmavalleypress.blogspot.co.uk